Emily Gravett

BEAR & HARE
Share!

Simon & Schuster Books for Young Readers

New York   London   Toronto   Sydney   New Delhi

Bear and Hare went for a walk.

Share?

asked Bear.

But Bear didn't care.

Bear and Hare
went for a walk.

Share?

asked Bear.

MINE !

said Hare.

But Bear didn't care.

Bear and Hare
went for a walk.

Oooh,
a balloon!

Share?

asked Bear.

MINE!

said Hare.

Bear and Hare went for a walk.

Ooh, honey!

But Bear was not there.

I DON'T CARE!

said Hare.

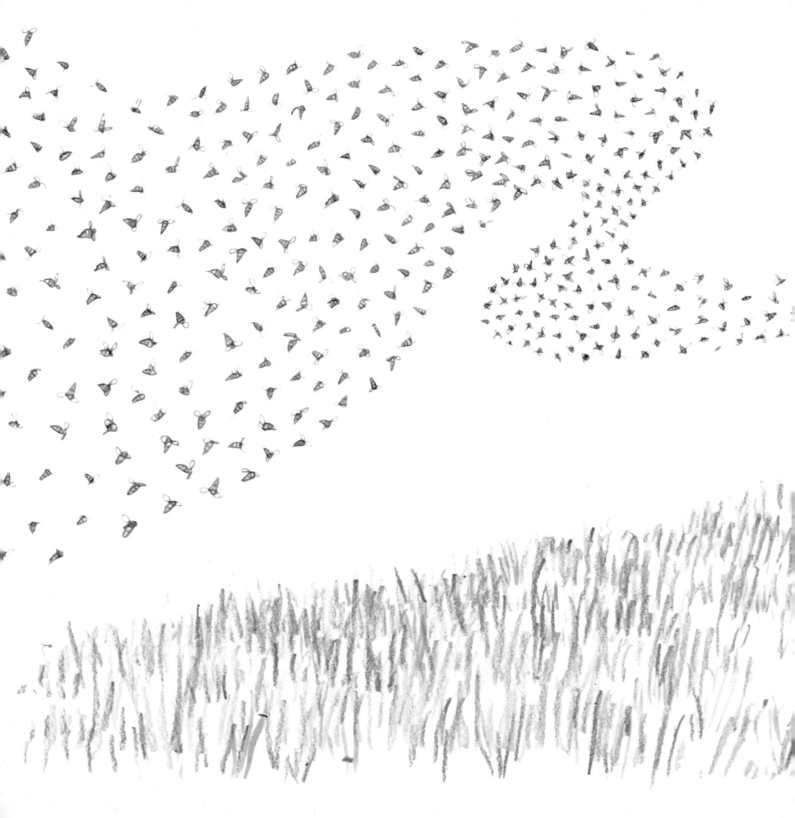

There there,

said Bear.

Share?

said Hare.

For Sonny